Sweetheart. Scandalous. Scummer.

OrangeBooks Publication

1st Floor, Rajhans Arcade, Mall Road, Kohka, Bhilai, Chhattisgarh 490020
Website: **www.orangebooks.in**

First Edition, 2026

ISBN: 978-93-7426-713-4

Price: Rs. 499.00

Printed in India

SWEETHEART.

SCANDALOUS. SCAMMER.

DR NISHANT S MEHTA

OrangeBooks Publication
www.orangebooks.in

"She scammed his heart.

He wrote her out of his story."

Dedication

To everyone who loved with their whole heart... and were met with silence, betrayal, or indifference. This is for the quiet cries, the deleted messages, the "maybe tomorrows"... and the strength it takes to walk away from someone you once begged to stay. You were never too much. They were just too little.

— Dr. Nishant S. Mehta

Author's Note

I did not write this book to vilify love, but to reveal its dangerous disguises. In an age where affection can be texted, ghosted, or gamed, emotional manipulation is one of the greatest cons we face.

Sweetheart. Scandalous. Scammer. is not just Arjun's story — it is a mirror for anyone who has ignored red flags, excused betrayal, or mistaken toxicity for love.

If there is one takeaway I wish for you, it is this: Your worth is not measured by who chooses to love you, but by how you learn to love yourself after being broken.

"Not every scam leaves a mark.

Some wear lipstick and say 'I love you.'"

Foreword

Life rarely moves in straight lines.

It twists, stumbles, dances in circles — and sometimes, it collapses under the weight of our own longing.

This is a story of Arjun, a man of profound decency and quiet dreams, who walked willingly into a storm named Maya. It is a tale spun from silken promises, torn by hidden betrayals, and stitched back together with fragile, trembling hope.

At its heart, *Sweetheart, Scandalous, Scammer* is not merely about love lost or trust shattered. It is about the unbearable beauty of being human — our desperate need to be chosen, to be seen, to be held close even when we are most unworthy. It explores how deeply we can drown in another's lies simply because we crave the illusion of forever.

But this story is also a hymn to resilience. To the way a wounded soul can learn to breathe again, to risk again, to stand naked in its vulnerability and still find the courage to love.

Along the way, there are stolen kisses, half-whispered confessions, nights heavy with regret, and mornings lit by tender, hesitant joy. There are moments that ache with erotic promise — only to reveal the cold void beneath. And then, there are moments of astonishing grace, when the universe seems to murmur, *"Start again, gentler this time."*

May this novel hold up a mirror to your own scars and remind you that even in your darkest hour, you are not alone. The heart — battered, betrayed, still foolishly hopeful — will find its way. It always does.

So, turn these pages with compassion. For Arjun. For Maya. For Isha.

And perhaps, most tenderly, for yourself.

— Dr. Nishant S. Mehta

Contents

Whispers of the Beginning

"Some heartbreaks aren't loud.
They whisper while you smile.

And bleed while you pretend to breathe."

Mumbai, October 2019

The rain hadn't stopped for three days. And yet, inside Arjun's modest yet elegant apartment on the 14th floor, everything felt dry — painfully so.

The ceiling fan creaked rhythmically as it sliced the thick, humid air. Books were scattered across the coffee table, legal files stacked neatly on the side. But his eyes weren't on the papers — they were fixed on a glowing rectangle. A WhatsApp screen. The message read: *"You there?"*

There was no reply.

He hadn't sent the message yet.

He never did.

Instead, he stared at the blinking cursor like it was some form of hope — a tiny heartbeat in the sea of digital detachment.

Arjun Mehra, 43, a respected **corporate lawyer** with a fierce courtroom presence and a limp that life had gifted him early, was not the kind of man who begged for attention. In the courtroom, his voice cut like a scalpel. But here, in the silence of his home, he longed to be heard.

What people saw was the success — a senior partner at a firm, known for his integrity, intellect, and the ability to shut down frauds worth crores.

What they missed was the ache. The soft, unspoken plea that had built up over the years: *"Choose me. Stay."*

The Voice Behind the Text

It began with a **LinkedIn comment.**

She had replied to a legal post he had shared — an article on ethical dilemmas in fintech audits. Most had liked it. She had critiqued it.

"Ethics without empathy becomes entitlement."

He was intrigued. Not offended.

Her name: **Maya Iyer.**

Her job title: *Vice President – Risk & Compliance, International*

Bank.

Her profile picture was muted — simple eyeliner, hair tied back, a pearl earring. Professional. But there was something defiant in her eyes.

Arjun had clicked 'Connect'. She accepted in ten minutes.

Then, came the first message:

"You write like you argue with yourself before arguing with the world."

He replied, smiling:

"And you comment like you're holding a mirror to strangers. Dangerous combination."

What started as playful banter turned into nightly conversations. Legal theories gave way to voice notes about chai, bad bosses, forgotten poems, and childhood insecurities.

He found himself waiting for her texts like he once waited for verdicts.

And she — she responded with a rhythm that was neither consistent nor absent. Just enough to keep him engaged. Never enough to let him feel secure.

The Soft Reveal

Over the next few weeks, Maya became a presence in his life — not physical, but hauntingly vivid.

She said she was raised by a strict mother.

She said she was "asexual by trauma," citing abuse by relatives. She confessed she found touch "triggering."

She shared screenshots of work pressure, of bosses gas lighting her, of being the only unmarried woman at her level.

Every message was a breadcrumb. Arjun followed.

He admired her — her sharpness, her empathy, her fire. But most of all, her vulnerability. She let him in, just enough.

They planned to meet.

She cancelled once because of a migraine. Then, because of her mother.

Then, because she was "not feeling herself."

He never pushed.

His patience wasn't strategy. It was love. Or at least, what he thought was love.

The Kiss That Never Was

There were moments — moments when it almost seemed real.

A voice note with her whispering "I wish I could hug you."

A selfie at midnight with a messy bun and no makeup captioned:

"If I let you see me like this, don't disappear."

And yet, when he asked to meet again, she ghosted for three days. When she returned, her excuse was typed, not spoken:

"I don't deserve someone like you. But I'm not ready to lose you either."

He didn't know whether to feel chosen… or cornered.

Why He Stayed

Arjun wasn't naïve. But he was lonely. There's a difference.

He had known touch — physical, fleeting, incomplete.

But what Maya gave him felt spiritual. Her pain became his purpose.

She called him "too good for this world." He called her "the chaos I choose."

Prelude to a Scam

It wasn't money. Not yet. It wasn't betrayal. Not yet.

It was… affection weaponized. Intimacy traded in scarcity.

She never asked him for much. Just his time. His words. His comfort.

But with each "I'm broken" she whispered, he gave her more of himself.

What he didn't know:

She wasn't building a relationship. She was building control.

And Arjun — the lawyer who knew how to expose truth in court — couldn't see the lie in front of him.

Because when you fall for someone's pain, you forget to question their story.

Chapter 1
Between Texts and Tea

"Sometimes, the worst heartbreaks are not from those who leave, but from those who stay... just enough to keep you hopeful."

December 2019 – Late Nights & Longing

For most of the city, December was wedding season — music, mehendis, marigolds.

For Arjun, it was the month of unread messages and overread memories.

Maya had now become a routine. Not in presence — in absence.

She never disappeared. She drifted.

Like fog. Like a promise just shy of fulfillment. A message at 2:11 AM:

"Can't sleep. Thinking about how fragile everything is."

A reply from Arjun at 2:12 AM:

"You're not fragile. You're just tired." And then... silence for 17 hours.

Digital Intimacy, Emotional Starvation

Every night, they shared something — an article, a photo, a broken thought.

Maya never sent selfies with a smile. Only moody glimpses: a half- lip in a mirror, a hand on a coffee mug, her feet on a yoga mat.

When Arjun once sent a photo of him with his law firm team, she replied:

"You look like someone who's used to pretending everything is okay."

He froze. She saw through him.

But she wouldn't let him see through her. He once asked:

"Do you believe in relationships?" Her answer:

"Only the ones that don't trap me."

And yet, she called him "my calm in chaos."

She spoke of being "safe" around him.

She'd say: "I don't want a boyfriend. I want a home. You feel like one."

He clung to those lines like oxygen.

The Meet That Didn't Happen

They had planned to meet again — this time for real.

A quiet dinner at her favorite place in Bandra. She even picked the day.

That morning, she messaged:

"Mom's blood pressure shot up. Can't leave her alone. I'm sorry."

He said he understood.

But he didn't.

He wore his best kurta anyway and sat alone at the sea-facing café for an hour, staring at the untouched second coffee cup he had ordered "just in case."

That night, Maya voice-noted him.

Her tone shaky, raw.

"Sometimes I think I'm cursed. Everyone I love either leaves me or breaks me. That's why I run before they do."

Arjun wanted to tell her — he wasn't going to run.

But somewhere deep inside, he also knew… she hadn't let him arrive.

The Illusion Deepens

She spoke of her trauma like postcards from hell — snapshots of abuse, betrayal, abandonment. But never the full picture.

"My uncle touched me when I was eight." "My ex hit me, but I told no one."

"My body feels foreign to me. I don't enjoy sex."

Each revelation was followed by withdrawal.

She would share something dark… then disappear.

It was a pattern.

When he tried to ask more, she replied:

"I'm not ready to relive all of it. Please don't make me."

So he didn't. He never asked again.

Instead, he sent poems.

He wrote her letters he never posted.

He mailed her a hardcover book she once mentioned in passing. She thanked him with a heart emoji.

No calls. No hugs. Just a pink heart on a blue screen.

When Giving Becomes a Habit

Arjun started adjusting his schedule around her replies.

He canceled dinners with friends to be available for her late-night pings.

He skipped Sunday badminton to help her "review a compliance policy" she sent for his legal opinion.

She said:

"You always know what to say."

But when he asked if she ever thought of him romantically, she typed:

"You're too pure. I don't want to ruin you." He didn't know what that meant.

Was it a compliment or rejection masked as concern?

The First Crack

One Sunday, she posted an Instagram story — a boomerang of a martini glass with the caption:

"Girls' night done right 🍸✨"

But he noticed something.

In the background, a man's voice — laughing. A familiar one.

He asked her about it. She replied:

"My brother dropped me. Chill. Not everything is drama."

He believed her.

Because he needed to.

But for the first time, he didn't sleep that night.

He just stared at his phone, wondering when he had begun to fear losing someone who wasn't even his.

The Red Flags He Painted White

Maya never asked for money.

But she did let him pay — for books, for cabs, for delivery dinners "on stressful days."

She called it sweet. He called it nothing.

It felt natural. She needed help. He had the means.

He was a lawyer. He dealt with people lying for a living.

But he never expected the woman who cried on voice notes to be one of them.

Because it's hard to suspect someone who claims to be broken. Even harder when they let you think you're the one fixing them.

Chapter 2
A Web Already Spun

There was a method to her madness.

Always had been.

From the outside, Maya appeared elegant, educated, and composed — a soft-spoken banker with just the right amount of mystery to be intriguing, and the right shade of vulnerability to be addictive.

But inside?

Inside, she was something else. Not evil.

Not broken.

Not a victim. Just... practiced.

It hadn't always been this way.

In college, Maya had loved purely. Once. A junior from a reputed law college in Bangalore — charming, intellectual, attentive. He made her believe in poems and promised Paris.

He broke her in silence.

Ghosted her for someone with clearer skin and clearer wealth.

Never gave a reason. Just vanished.

She didn't cry for long. She studied.

Not books.

People.

She learned how some men responded to silence like dogs to a whistle.

She learned that a faint smile on a video call could soften a hardened businessman in Dubai.

She learned that being *almost* available was more powerful than being fully there.

"Give a man a fantasy…then disappear.

He'll chase you for the rest of the month."

And so, she built her algorithm — Not of code,

But of emotion.

There was the CA from Indore.

The startup bro from Hyderabad.

The gym-obsessed banker from Gurgaon.

The photographer from Pune who offered to tattoo her name.

They were never all active at once.

No — she was far too disciplined for that. She rotated affection like portfolios.

Some were emotional investors.

Some were ATMs with a crush.

Some were stepping stones.

But then came Arjun.

Arjun was different. Not because he was special. But because he was dangerous.

He had the two things most men didn't have together: **Emotion** and **resources**.

He remembered her coffee order.

He noticed when she changed her lipstick shade.

He remembered her fake stories about a strict mother and an invisible curfew.

But more importantly —

He paid attention.

Too much of it.

That scared her.

But also... intrigued her.

Could she control him?

Could she make him dance — not just with words, but with longing?

Could she become the obsession that no other woman could replace?

She decided to try.

First, she gave him softness —

Late-night calls where she whispered her "fears."

"I'm asexual," she said once. "Hope you won't judge me." He didn't.

Then came the trauma tales. An "ex" who crossed a line. A "friend" who betrayed her.

She let a tear form, let it fall only once, and then laughed it off. "Anyway, that's the past. I'm healing."

She wrapped her wounds in velvet. She made her silence look sacred. She made denial look like depth.

Arjun offered himself in full.

Time.

Money.

Heart.

She took it all like it was her right.

She told herself she was only doing what life had done to her.

That she was just reversing the game.

But deep down, she knew better.

During the brief breakup — when Arjun had sensed the coldness in her voice — she had already started texting an ex.

Just casually.

The "good morning"s returned.

The late-night nostalgia games began.

She told him about Arjun — not the name, but the type. *"He's sweet. Overly sweet. Like cake after a heartbreak."* Then came the hotel day.

She knew she didn't love Arjun.

Not like that.

But he was convenient. And devoted. And capable of giving her a lifestyle she craved.

So she gave him just enough — A hug too long,

A kiss too warm,

A smile too sincere.

She whispered "I love you" with eyes that didn't blink.

A moment of illusion is all it takes to buy three more months of loyalty.

She had planned Bhutan even before the hospital lie. Even before asking for ₹3,00,000.

She just hadn't booked it yet.

She watched him hesitate only for a second before transferring the funds.

She smiled to herself.

Another test passed.

Maya had no fixed plan for Arjun. She didn't want to marry him.

She didn't even want a long-term affair. She just wanted to be adored.

Unquestioned. Unchallenged. Uninterrupted.

And when the adoration faded — She'd walk.

Softly. Quietly. Beautifully.

Just like always.

He was not her first.

He would not be her last.

But for a while,

He was the most profitable one.

Chapter 3

Strings from the Shadows

It was a quiet Thursday afternoon — one of those rare days when the city paused, and Arjun found himself craving a conversation with Maya.

She hadn't replied to his morning texts. No blue ticks. No "good morning baby 🌞", no memes, no passive-aggressive emojis. It wasn't like her.

He tried calling. Once. Twice. Straight to voicemail.

By late afternoon, concern was crawling up his spine. He messaged again.

"Everything okay? Just checking in."

An hour later, she replied.

"Ma got a heart attack. Rushing to hospital." His breath hitched. "What?! Where are you?" *"On the way. Don't call. Will update."*

He froze for a moment, then immediately offered, *"Should I book a flight? I'll get you there. Just send me details."*

Her reply came a few minutes later.

"Wait. Going with my brother. Will fly to Indore from Delhi tonight."

Something felt off. The tone was mechanical. No panic. No breakdown. Just... updates.

But Arjun silenced the doubt.

She's in shock. Don't make this about you. Support her.

He kept checking his phone through the evening, praying for a message, a ping, a word. By nightfall — silence.

By the next morning — nothing.

He messaged again. No reply.

Hours passed.

No blue ticks.

By late evening, she responded.

"Mom's in ICU. Critical. I'm really scared. I'm with dad and bhaiya."

Arjun's heart sank. "I'm here for you. Anything you need," he texted.

There was no response after that.

And then — complete silence.

Three full days passed. Not a single message. No updates. No calls. No social media. Nothing.

She had disappeared, leaving behind a silent storm that only he was drowning in.

On the fourth morning, his phone rang.

Her name blinked on screen. He felt his heart jolt.

"Hey," she whispered, voice low and fragile. "Maya? How are you? How's your mom?"

She paused. "Still in ICU… Arjun, I… I need some help." His voice softened. "Anything. Tell me."

She took a deep breath. "I'm short of funds. Mom's debit card is with me, and there's an issue withdrawing. I need to clear some immediate bills. I didn't want to ask bhaiya or dad. I'll return it soon, I promise."

"How much?" He asked gently.

"Three lakhs." Three lakhs.

No hospital name.

No screenshot. No formal bill. Just the ask.

But he didn't blink.

Within two minutes, he had opened his banking app, initiated the transfer, and messaged her the confirmation.

She sent a "Thank you. I owe you big time."

And that was it.

Over the next few days, the silence returned. A few check-ins here and there, a "still hectic" here, a "too tired to talk" there. But no calls. No voice notes. No warmth.

Then, like a ghost reappearing in daylight, she pinged one evening:

"Hey! Guess what — going to Bhutan with family next week! Can't wait □✨"

Arjun's screen froze.

Bhutan?

"Your mom... is okay now?" He typed slowly.

"Yeah, recovering well! She wanted a break. I planned the whole trip. Everything sorted now!"

He didn't know what to say.

So he said nothing.

She flooded his inbox with photos over the next week — smiling selfies, snow-capped mountains, yak trails, luxury hotel rooms, bonfire videos. All curated. All vibrant.

He replied with the occasional emoji. He tried to be polite. Detached. Distant. But inside, he was breaking.

A few days into her trip, he remembered that she had once shared her bank statement with him — for some consulting help he had offered.

He opened it out of curiosity, intending nothing — just to see if everything had been sorted.

And then he saw it.

The very same day he had sent the ₹3,00,000 — There was no transaction to any hospital.

No ICU.

No medical expense.

Instead, there were entries to a travel booking portal, a boutique resort in Bhutan, and an airline ticketing site.

His fingers trembled.

He checked the date again. He checked the amount.

Everything matched.

She hadn't gone to pay her mother's bills. She had gone to book her own escape.

He sat back.

Staring at the screen. Then at the ceiling. Then nowhere.

He didn't scream.

He didn't message her. He didn't confront.

He just... paused.

Sometimes betrayal doesn't arrive with a knife. It arrives wearing lipstick, Holding a phone,

Smiling in photos

You paid for.

He went silent.

Even when she returned from Bhutan and resumed her bubbly texts.

Even when she sent selfies and said, *"Missed talking to you!"*

He smiled back. Emoji. Thumbs up. But inside, a new version of him was being born.

The one who loved her — was fading.

And the one who knew the truth — was learning to live with it.

Chapter 4
Kisses, Excuses, & Illusions

"Sometimes, it's not the absence of touch that hurts.

It's being close enough to feel the warmth—and still not allowed in."

January 2020 – The Kiss That Didn't Mean

The first time Maya let Arjun kiss her was on a quiet weekday night.

She had called him to meet her near her office in Lower Parel. It was already past 9. He had court the next morning. But when she said,

"I just want to sit somewhere and not talk to anyone," he was already in his car, navigating the traffic, heart racing like a teenager.

They didn't go anywhere fancy. Just sat on Marine Drive, sharing a paper plate of chaat, her heels off, her eyes distant.

For the first fifteen minutes, she said nothing. Then suddenly: "Why are you nice to me, Arjun? I don't deserve it."

He didn't have an answer. He just smiled and wiped her tears with the sleeve of his court shirt.

She leaned in and kissed him.

Softly. Briefly. But with a sadness that felt rehearsed. It wasn't the kind of kiss you remember for the thrill.

It was the kind you remember because it left you colder after. When she pulled away, she whispered:

"Sorry. I just needed to feel something human."

Not a Relationship. A Ritual.

After that, Arjun thought things would progress. They didn't.

Maya never called it dating. She refused labels.

"We're energy. Don't box this into boyfriend-girlfriend drama," she said once.

They'd meet once every week or two. Always on her terms. Sometimes in cafés. Sometimes parked in his car. Once even outside a bookstore that was about to shut.

She allowed small touches — holding hands, brushing shoulders—but flinched if he moved in closer.

He once tried to wrap his arm around her shoulder. She stiffened.

"Please… I don't like being touched unexpectedly."

He apologised. Repeatedly. But it lingered in his mind.

Why would someone initiate a kiss one day and recoil the next? She had explanations. Always.

"I told you, I'm asexual." "Sex makes me feel dirty."

"My mom would freak if she found out I was with someone."

"My past messed me up. I'm not like other girls." He accepted every reason like gospel.

The Shopping and the Silence

Maya started sending him screenshots of things she wanted — perfumes, clothes, shoes — followed by emojis and:

"Would look good on me?"

He always responded:

"Definitely. Want me to order it?" She never asked directly.

But she never refused either.

Slowly, she became more present digitally and less available physically.

"I have work."

"Mom's acting weird."

"My therapist says I need space."

Yet she'd send selfies in a towel robe after a spa day or a pouty boomerang with a caption like *"Messy bun, still getting it done."*

It kept Arjun hooked — guessing, waiting, hoping.

The Three-Month Freeze

By March, she had almost stopped meeting him altogether.

Excuses flowed like water.

Her bank had a new compliance deadline. Her cousin was getting married.

She had mood swings. She had therapy.

She had to help her mom.

But the online chats never stopped.

She'd ask about his day, his dog, his parents' anniversary. She even remembered his courtroom win and texted:

"Your brain is so sexy. You'll win SC cases someday."

It was like emotional foreplay with no promise of closeness.

He asked her if she was angry with him. She replied:

"No, silly. I'm just messed up. You deserve better."

But she never let him leave either.

The Rise of Confusion

One evening, after 17 days of not meeting, Arjun tried calling her.

No answer.

Then a message:

"Can't talk. At spa with Ma."

Hours later, she posted a reel — she was clearly at a high-end bar, the kind Arjun couldn't afford, sipping cocktails and laughing with someone whose hand appeared briefly in the frame.

When Arjun messaged her about it, she replied with a string of emojis and:

"Wow. You stalking my life now? Relax. It's just a friend."

He felt small.

Stupid.

But the next morning, she sent him a Spotify playlist titled:

"You see me when I hide."

The first track: "Liability" by Lorde. The last: "Fix You" by Coldplay.

And just like that, Arjun was drawn back in.

When Reality Begins to Blur

By April, their connection had no rhythm.

No intimacy.

No definition.

Only dependency.

He tried pulling back.

She'd send a photo of her eyes crying. He'd call. She wouldn't pick up.

Then three hours later:

"You're the only one I trust. Don't give up on me."

She had mastered the art of vanishing — right before he needed clarity — and reappearing when she sensed him letting go.

He knew something was wrong.

But he couldn't define it.

And Maya knew — the hardest prisons are the ones without bars.

Chapter 5
The Proposal That Wasn't

"Some invitations are not made of words — they're sewn in silence and sealed with illusion."

April 2020 – The Suggestion Wrapped in Fantasy

They were sitting in Arjun's car. The windows fogged slightly, the Mumbai drizzle weaving patterns like forgotten constellations on the glass. It had been one of those rare evenings when Maya agreed to meet — a short coffee catch-up that Arjun had turned into a date in his mind, though it barely lasted an hour.

As she stared into her latte, suddenly, as if speaking to herself, she said,

"Sometimes I wish I could just leave… go somewhere where no one knows me."

Arjun looked up, curious. "Where would you go?"

A pause. A glint in her eye.

"London. Always dreamt of it. The old bookstores, the cobbled streets, the rain that doesn't feel like Mumbai's chaos."

She smiled softly, her eyes somewhere else.

"Maybe I should just take a break and disappear for a while."

He didn't respond immediately. Something in her tone felt like a test.

Then she said it:

"You know… if you ever feel like running away too, we could go.

Just you and me. Like a little honeymoon... without the marriage." His heart skipped.

A Dream He Wasn't Allowed to Dream

For days after, Arjun replayed that sentence.

A honeymoon without the marriage.

He wasn't sure what she meant — but he didn't care. The idea of being with her for more than stolen hours, waking up in the same timezone, seeing her smile without Wi-Fi delays — it was intoxicating.

He offered to plan it.

She laughed.

"You and your spreadsheets. Let me plan something impulsive for once."

He agreed.

She took charge.

The flights were business class. The Airbnb was a stylish flat near Southbank. Her wishlist included Harrods, Notting Hill, afternoon teas, and one peculiar request:

"We must go to the Kew Gardens. I've read it's healing for broken souls."

Arjun didn't even ask about the budget. He transferred ₹5 lakhs without blinking. Then another ₹10 lakhs.

"Just make it magical," he texted.

She replied:

"You already have."

Romance in Theory

In the buildup to the trip, Maya's tone softened. For the first time, she sent him a selfie of herself in bed — no makeup, tousled hair, a pillow over half her face.

"Missing you," it read.

Arjun saved the photo. Looked at it every night.

She also shared more personal things: her father's anger, her mother's orthodox restrictions, a shadowy story of abuse that came out late one night when Arjun was half-asleep on call.

"I was violated… by someone in the family. That's why I can't be touched sometimes."

He froze. Whispered apologies. Wanted to hold her.

She hung up abruptly that night.

"I can't talk about this. Don't ask me again."

He never did.

Instead, he began preparing to be gentler. Kinder. To protect her.

Even if she never said the words, he believed it: this trip was their beginning.

Everything, Except the Emotion

Just days before the flight, she sent a list of things she wanted to shop for "in advance":

- A Burberry trench for her "brother"
- A Fossil wallet
- Men's loafers
- Giorgio Armani fragrance

"He's always there for me. Want to surprise him," she said casually. Arjun paid.

He felt uneasy.

"Your brother? The same one you said you don't speak to much?" She brushed it off.

"It's complicated. But he's blood. And no, I don't love him. Don't overthink." He dropped it. He always did.

The Farewell Before the Illusion

The night before they flew, Arjun packed Maya's cosmetics and sandals in his suitcase — she said hers was overflowing.

They didn't meet that night.

"Too much to do. Mom is crying already. Don't want her to curse me."

Still, she sent a voice note:

"I hope this trip changes us. But please — be patient with me if I get weird."

He cried listening to it.

His bags were heavy with hope.

Departure

At the airport, she wore a grey hoodie, no makeup, hair in a bun. Arjun thought she looked beautiful.

She didn't hold his hand. Didn't smile much.

Seemed on edge.

"Are you okay?" He asked.

"Just leave me alone till we land. I hate flights."

He nodded.

In the air, while he stared out the window at stars, she plugged in her Air Pods and slept away from him.

Still, Arjun believed: once they reached London, once she felt free—everything would finally begin. He didn't know…

It was already ending.

Chapter 6

The Afternoon That Almost Changed Everything

"Some moments feel like magic. Until you realize — they were rehearsals, not memories."

It started with a message that Arjun read twice before believing.

Maya: *"I was thinking... I could come over for a bit. Maybe we spend a few hours together. You can book a hotel or something?"*

No disclaimers. No trauma-laced warnings. No reference to her mother watching her every move or her body rejecting physical touch.

Just a gentle offer wrapped in ellipses.

Arjun's heart stuttered. Not from lust, but from disbelief.

Was this the same Maya who once said she didn't believe in sex?

The same woman who had turned away after kisses, whose tears arrived faster than her touch, who had built walls of trauma and sworn she'd never let anyone in?

And yet — here she was. Suggesting time. Alone. Together. His fingers hesitated over the keyboard.

Arjun: *"Are you sure?"*

Her reply came with a voice note.

"I don't know. Maybe I'm feeling reckless today. You make me feel safe. Let's just make some memories... no overthinking."

It wasn't a green light. It was amber — flickering with hope, caution, and possibility.

But Arjun was tired of waiting at red lights. He decided to go all in.

He booked the best hotel in Mumbai. A suite at *The Elanora.* Known for its skyline views, velvet furniture, and a scent that always lingered between seduction and serenity. The kind of place where billionaires closed deals — or broke hearts.

He requested rose petals. Scented candles. A strawberry cheesecake with the words:

"You are my first. My always."

A bit dramatic, he thought. But today, he didn't care.

He even asked the concierge to play soft instrumental music before their arrival.

As he picked her up that afternoon — she was already glowing. A different kind of glow. She had just received her first car delivery that morning, a gift he had helped arrange, and she rode high on that cloud of pride and excitement.

"Your car suits you," Arjun smiled as she buckled in. "You mean classy and a little complicated?" She teased.

He laughed. But there was something else in her voice today — not mockery, not distance. Just lightness. Warmth.

When they pulled up at the hotel entrance, she looked up in awe. "This is Elanora?! Arjun, this place is... wow," she whispered.

As they stepped inside the marble-floored lobby, her fingers brushed his. She didn't flinch. She didn't pull away.

For the first time in months, he felt not like a man waiting on love—but like one receiving it.

They checked in, walked down a quiet corridor, and entered the suite.

The room was bathed in golden light. Soft jazz played from the ceiling speakers. Fresh lilies framed the windows. The cake hadn't yet arrived, nor the balloons—but the warmth of the room made up for it.

Maya turned in a slow circle and clapped her hands like a child.

"You did all this?" She asked, eyes wide.

"For you," he said simply.

And then — she hugged him. Tight. Without hesitation. Without fear.

"I love you," she whispered into his shirt.

Three words he had waited for. Not in message bubbles. Not in evasive poems. But here. Out loud. In his arms.

His chest rose with gratitude. His fingers stroked her hair. He kissed her forehead. Her cheek. Her lips.

And this time — she kissed back. Fully.

Hungrily.

The next hour unfolded like a scene from a memory that had waited years to be written.

They undressed each other slowly, awkwardly, tenderly.

She laughed when his hands fumbled with her bra clasp. He whispered a joke about never learning the mechanism in law school.

She blushed when he looked at her fully — the first time he saw her without layers, not just of clothing, but of fear. She stood there, bare and vulnerable, covering nothing.

"You're staring," she said softly.

"You're... beautiful," he replied, barely breathing.

They made their way to the bed. The sheets were cool. The world outside faded.

He touched her gently — not as a man claiming, but as a man cherishing. She responded with soft moans, sighs that sounded like surrender.

For the first time, she allowed everything — her body, her laughter, her neck arched back in pleasure.

But then, just when it was time — when passion crested into intimacy — she paused.

Arjun noticed it instantly. Her breath shortened. Her grip loosened. Her eyes darted away.

“Are you okay?” He asked, concerned.

“I want to,” she whispered. “I really do.” But her body tensed.

He leaned back, calmed his breath. “It’s okay. We don’t have to. This doesn’t have to happen today.”

She looked disappointed. Not at him — at herself.

“I wanted this to be perfect,” she said. “But I don’t know what’s wrong with me.”

“There’s nothing wrong with you,” Arjun said, holding her hand. “This isn’t the last time. We have time.”

But somewhere in his mind, something whispered — *Then why does it feel like this might be the only time?*

Later, she changed into the white satin bathrobe provided by the hotel.

She stepped onto the balcony with a wine glass in hand and smiled at the skyline.

“Thanks for today,” she said. “You made me feel... something again.”

They clicked photos together — smiling selfies, kiss-on-the-cheek poses, a picture of the cake when it finally arrived.

Then, lying beside each other on the bed, he asked casually, "If we could go anywhere — just the two of us—where would you want to go?"

She smiled.

Didn't answer.

Instead, she opened her phone, scrolled through her gallery, and pulled up a wallpaper — the iconic *London Eye*, lit up against the twilight sky.

"This," she said, turning the screen to him.

"You've always wanted to go to London?" He asked.

"Always," she nodded. "For the bookstores. And the rain. It feels... romantic. Healing."

He leaned in and kissed her again.

"Then we'll go. You and me. London."

She smiled, kissed his cheek, and curled into him.

But even as she did — her eyes stayed open a little longer than usual.

Her smile lasted just one second too short. And Arjun didn't know…

That this moment — this beautiful, imperfect, tender afternoon—would be the last time she let him close enough to feel wanted. Because London wasn't a dream.

It was already a plan.

Just not one that included him.

Chapter 7
The Calm Before the Storm

"The deepest betrayals don't shout. They sip tea with you, smile, and promise forever."

In the days that followed that tender afternoon at Elanora, Arjun felt something inside him ease — a knot finally untangled, a page finally turned. That afternoon had not just been about touch or desire, but about validation.

She had said it.

"I love you."

And she had let him in — into her body, into her breath, into that hidden place she had always guarded with excuses of trauma and reluctance.

He told himself: *This is it. We've crossed the line between longing and becoming.*

And yet, within just seventy-two hours, that certainty began to fray.

Maya didn't vanish.

No. That would've been obvious.

Instead, she softened her presence — like turning down a dimmer on a light that once burned too bright.

Her messages still came, but they felt filtered — like she was editing herself in real-time. The timing changed too. Where once she would voice note him past midnight, whispering poems and anxiety and unfiltered emotion, now she replied at 3 p.m. or 5:30 p.m. with "Haha" and "Hmm" and "You're overthinking."

Even her voice notes had a strange air — like she was reading a script. Familiar words, unfamiliar energy.

Arjun noticed it, of course.

He was a lawyer, trained to hear what wasn't said. He had built his career exposing frauds, decoding silence, and spotting deception wrapped in legalese.

But when it came to Maya, he silenced the part of himself that had always known better.

He asked her one evening, "Can we meet this weekend? Even if just for coffee."

Her reply took four hours.

"Ma's been unwell again. BP issues. Can't leave her alone. Sorry, love."

The word *"love"* should've comforted him. But it felt... thrown in. Like seasoning added to a bland dish after it's already cooked.

He let it go.

Then asked, “Can I come see you at your place? Just for five minutes?”

“Haha, are you crazy? My mom would kill me. And I look like a mess today. Let’s video call instead.”

And they did. But the calls became shorter. Less intimate. She would multitask — folding clothes, replying to emails, checking notifications mid-conversation.

Once, while he was telling her about an intense courtroom case, she interrupted:

“Sorry, can I call you back? My brother is calling.”

That brother again.

The mysterious, ever-present *bhaiyya* who never made it into her stories, but seemed to appear whenever Arjun asked for her time.

He smiled. Nodded. Hung up.

And sat staring at the screen, wondering when he started competing with ghosts.

A few nights later, Maya sent him a photo.

She wore a white T-shirt, hair in a messy bun, eyes lined dark and dramatic. It was captioned:

“This look okay for an engagement party? Just attending, not starring. Haha.”

He froze.

Engagement.

His fingers trembled as he typed:

"Whose engagement?"

She replied casually:

"A friend. Distant relative. Too much bling, not enough soul."

He didn't ask more.

But something about the way she had styled herself… the lipstick, the subtle shimmer in her eye makeup, the new necklace… it didn't look like someone dressing for a distant relative.

It looked like someone getting *seen.* The next evening, he called again. She didn't pick up.

Instead, she sent a photo — a framed shot of a slice of chocolate cake and a glass of wine on a plush velvet table.

"Celebrating alone. Cheers to small wins."

He replied:

"Wish I was there."

She didn't respond.

The next morning, he tried to shake it off.

Maybe she was just overwhelmed. Maybe he was reading into things again.

And yet, something inside him — a buried voice long muffled — began to tap louder.

Something isn't right.

Then came the strangest moment of all.

They were on a video call late one night — a call that felt more like a check-in than a conversation. Maya's face was dimly lit, the angle slightly off, her voice distant.

He noticed a velvet ring box on the dresser behind her.

It sat there — unapologetically visible — as if daring him to notice.

He said nothing. Neither did she.

Instead, she talked about a new compliance policy her boss had screwed up, then showed him a pair of earrings she had ordered online.

The box stayed in the frame for a full ten minutes. Then, casually, she shifted her camera.

And just like that, it was gone.

That night, Arjun wrote in his journal:

"She isn't lying outright. But she's not telling the truth either. She floats between words — never giving you enough to hold, never saying enough to prove. You're left guessing. Always guessing. And still, you stay."

Days passed.

He asked again, "Let's meet this Sunday? I'll plan something." *"Let's not plan. Let's just... be. Planning kills spontaneity."* He tried one last time.

"Are we still us, Maya?"

She replied almost instantly.

"You're doing that thing again — turning something beautiful into pressure. Let's not ruin it."

Pressure.

That word stabbed deeper than he expected. How had wanting clarity become pressure?

And then, one night, out of nowhere — she lit up.

On call, she looked radiant. Eyes bright, laughter easy.

"Guess what?" She said, turning her phone toward the ceiling. "What?" He asked, smiling despite himself.

She scrolled to a picture on her gallery.

The *London Eye.*

Its lights twinkling against a dusky lavender sky.

"This," she said softly. "Let's go here. Just you and me. No stress.

No rules."

His heart thudded in joy.

"London?" She nodded.

"You really mean it?"

"I do," she whispered. "Let's make memories before life makes excuses."

Arjun didn't sleep that night.

He researched flights. Booked premium seats. Paid for an Airbnb she had picked — a stylish flat near Southbank.

When the total cost came up to over ₹15 lakhs — he didn't flinch. This wasn't a vacation.

This was *finally happening.*

They were in love.

They were going to London.

They were beginning their forever.

But what he didn't know…

Was that she had already begun her goodbye.

And the only luggage she carried heavier than her shopping bags… Was her silence.

Chapter 8
London Lies – Part I

The airplane shuddered softly as it cut through the grey British skies.

Arjun looked out the window, the clouds breaking over a city he had once only dreamed of visiting with someone he loved. Now, he was here — with her. With Maya. His heartbeat was light. The seatbelt still pressed against his lap as the wheels kissed the Heathrow tarmac.

She sat beside him, eyes closed, her head resting against the seat, earbuds in. Calm. Unbothered. Beautiful.

Arjun, meanwhile, couldn't help but whisper to himself:

"This is it.

This is the trip.

The beginning of us. Really us."

The immigration lines were long, but Maya breezed through them like a seasoned traveller. Arjun followed, lugging her carry-on suitcase in addition to his own. She didn't stop to thank him — not rudely, just... absent-mindedly.

He chalked it up to excitement.

They stepped out into the chill of a London evening. A private taxi was already waiting — pre-booked by Arjun. He had chosen a boutique hotel near Westminster, not too flashy, but elegant, with floral wallpaper and modern interiors. Maya had seen photos of it on WhatsApp and had replied with a single word: *"Cute."*

It had meant the world to him.

The hotel receptionist smiled as they checked in. Maya gave a polite nod, barely looking at Arjun. When they entered their room — an intimate suite with a view of the London Eye — she threw herself onto the bed, arms wide.

"It's nice," she said. "Very Instagrammable."

She took out her phone and began snapping selfies. Arjun stood at the doorway, watching her.

Something felt... off.

She was here, but not really present. Beside him, but not with him.

Still, he told himself not to overthink.

Later that night, they walked down Southbank.

London glistened — the kind of city that made you believe anything was possible. Street musicians played soft jazz. A couple kissed in a corner. The Thames flowed steadily, unaware of the stories it silently carried.

Arjun reached out for Maya's hand.

She let him hold it — but only for a minute. Then, she slipped her fingers away, tucking her hand into her coat.

"It's cold," she said flatly.

And just like that, the warmth vanished.

Dinner was at Dishoom.

He had made a reservation weeks in advance, even ordered her favorite black daal and okra fries. Maya looked stunning smoky eyes, wine-red lipstick, and a beige trench coat. Heads turned when she walked in.

But throughout the meal, she kept checking her phone.

Once, she even stepped away, saying she needed to take a call from her mom. Arjun nodded.

But a part of him burned.

Mom.

Always the mom.

The invisible wall she hid behind.

When she returned, her tone was lighter. She scrolled through Instagram stories, chuckled at a meme, and leaned forward.

"Let's go shopping tomorrow, na? Oxford Street?" Her voice had honey now.

Arjun nodded, the ache in his chest softening. Maybe he was just overthinking.

That night, in the hotel, he lit a candle — one he had carried from India, a vanilla-sandalwood blend. He set it near the window, hoping to create a soft, romantic vibe.

Maya was in the bathroom, freshening up.

He dimmed the lights. Adjusted the pillows. Took out the small gift he had wrapped — a delicate pendant with her initials and a tiny silver heart.

When she came out, wrapped in a towel, her hair wet, face scrubbed clean — Arjun smiled.

“You look... like magic,” he said.

She gave a faint smile. Walked over to the window.

“London is beautiful,” she whispered.

He reached out, gently taking her hand again. This time, she didn’t resist.

He leaned in for a kiss. She let him. A long, slow kiss.

But when he pulled her closer, trying to deepen the moment, she pulled away.

“Not tonight. I’m tired,” she said, already turning toward the bed.

Tired.

Again.

Like every other time.

Arjun sat still for a while, watching her scroll through her phone even as the candle flickered quietly beside them.

He placed the gift box back into his bag.

Unopened. Unseen.

As she fell asleep with her back to him, Arjun whispered:

"I brought my heart across continents. You brought silence."

But the next morning, Maya was sunshine again.

Playful. Laughing. Asking for croissants. Making him pose with double-decker buses.

She kissed him on the cheek outside a café. For a few hours, the shadows disappeared. But Arjun didn't know…

That this trip — this dream he had saved for, prayed for, planned with all his heart — would become the beginning of his unraveling.

Because Maya wasn't just hiding behind excuses anymore. She was already planning her next chapter —

One that didn't include him.

Chapter 9
The Games Behind the Glass

London had never looked so bright. Or so blurred.

The morning after that half-kiss, half-goodbye night, Arjun convinced himself to reset. A new day, a new start. After all, this was the city of love, of new beginnings. He'd flown across the world not just for her—but for them.

They stood outside Selfridges as Maya posed next to a designer store window, her lips pursed, sunglasses oversized. She wasn't smiling, but she looked good. Arjun, holding three shopping bags, waited nearby.

She didn't want photos with him. Just photos for him to click.

"Should we grab some lunch?" He asked.

Maya was typing a message on her phone. "You go ahead and grab coffee. I'll check out the next floor. There's a sale on."

Arjun nodded.

Not once had she said, *"Let's go together."*

Not once had she reached for his hand. An hour passed.

Then two.

She hadn't returned to the café where he waited. No messages. No calls.

Finally, he texted her.

"Still at Selfridges?"

Her reply came 10 minutes later.

"Was on a call. Coming down now."

When she appeared, she was smiling — not at him, but at her phone.

He saw the screen just for a second.

A man's face on a WhatsApp call screen.

"Bro ❤" it said.

His stomach twisted.

Bro.

That same word she once used to describe someone else. The one she got engaged to later.

But he said nothing.

Instead, he stood and smiled like a fool. Paid for her coffee. Opened the cab door. Let her sit inside.

They went to the London Eye that evening.

She had mentioned it months ago — even had a wallpaper of it. Arjun had booked two VIP tickets. No queues, private pod, champagne.

Inside the glass pod, the city sprawled beneath them. Dusk painted the Thames in blush gold.

Arjun turned to her.

"Thank you for coming with me."

She looked at him, slightly confused. "You booked the trip."

He laughed nervously. "Yes, but... you agreed. That means more than you think."

She took a sip of her drink and leaned against the glass.

"I didn't know it'd be this cold in London," she said, arms wrapped around herself.

He offered his jacket. She refused.

Always this dance —

One step close, Two steps back.

Halfway through the ride, he turned to her again. "Do you ever think about what this means?" "What?"

"Us. Being here. Traveling together."

She paused. "It's nice. But let's not overthink, Arjun. This is a good phase. Just live it."

Phase.

Not a journey. Not a beginning. Just... a phase.

He swallowed the ache.

Later that night, he booked a special dinner cruise on the Thames.

Fairy lights, jazz, fine wine. Maya looked stunning in her dark green evening dress. Arjun couldn't stop looking at her — her eyes, her silence, her perfect distance.

They danced once.

She let him hold her close — but she never met his eyes.

On the ride back to the hotel, she leaned against the car window, humming a tune softly.

He turned to her. "Maya, I feel like... I'm always trying. But I don't know if you're here with me."

She didn't reply immediately.

Instead, she said, "You're overthinking again. I'm just not expressive. You know that."

"But are you… happy?" He asked. "Yes. Don't make this difficult."

She closed her eyes. Conversation over. That night, they slept back-to-back. Again.

He wanted to talk. She wanted sleep.

He wanted a moment. She wanted a story for Instagram.

The next morning, she woke up cheerful. "Let's go to Notting Hill today. I want those pretty street photos."

Arjun smiled, hiding his tiredness. "Of course. Anything you want."

They walked through pastel-colored houses. She took dozens of photos. Arjun held her bags, her coat, her coffee cup.

A street performer played "Let Her Go" on the guitar.

"Only know you love her when you let her go…"

He looked at Maya — smiling at her own reflection in a shop window.

He whispered:

"I don't want to let you go.

But I'm starting to lose you anyway."

That night, he tried again.

"I got us show tickets tomorrow. Phantom of the Opera. You once mentioned you love music."

"Oh, you remembered," she said, mildly surprised. He smiled. "I remember everything."

She looked down.

"I might have dinner with an old friend. From uni. Just for an hour or so."

Of course.

The invisible friend.

Another convenient ghost from the past.

Arjun nodded.

He was learning to stop asking questions.

He sat on the edge of the hotel bed later that evening, alone, scrolling through their photos.

Most were of her. None were of them. He opened Instagram.

She had posted a story: "London vibes ❤"

No tags. No mention. Just her.

Always just her.

Chapter 10

Hotel Rooms and Hidden Truths

The evening lights of London felt colder now.

Arjun sat on the edge of the hotel bed, laptop open but untouched. A steaming cup of chamomile tea sat beside him, getting colder by the minute — like most things in this trip.

Maya had stepped out hours ago — supposedly to meet an "old college friend" for dinner. He had offered to join. She had said, *"It's just catching up. I'll be back soon."*

Soon.

Such a dangerous word. Too long to wait.

Too short to fight.

It was nearly 10:30 PM. No sign of her.

He refreshed WhatsApp. No blue ticks. No typing indicator. No missed calls.

He scrolled through Instagram, half hoping she wouldn't have posted anything.

But there it was — a boomerang.

Her glass clinking with another. A cozy wine bar. Candlelight.

No friend in the frame. Just two hands.

One of them wasn't his.

He stared at it until his screen dimmed.

Then he stood up and walked toward the window.

The view was magnificent — the London Eye glowing in the distance. Tourists milled below. The world was still spinning.

But for him — everything had stopped.

He brought his love

To this city of lights.

She brought her silence

And left him in the shadows.

She returned close to midnight.

Laughing on the phone as she entered, her voice coated in honey.

She looked surprised to see him still awake.

"Oh… hey. You're still up?"

He smiled faintly. "I couldn't sleep."

She took off her coat, dropped her handbag on the side chair, and walked past him like he wasn't there.

Like a ghost.

Invisible.

Present in the room, absent in the heart.

He wanted to ask her where she was.

Who she was with. Why she hadn't texted.

But he didn't.

Instead, he asked, "Did you have fun?"

She nodded. "Yeah. Good catching up. I didn't eat much though. Can we order room service?"

He blinked.

"You want dinner now?"

She grinned. "Yeah. Just something light."

He called down, ordered pasta and soup, and watched her slip into the bathroom.

While she was gone, he glanced at her phone. It was face-down. Locked. Silenced.

He didn't dare touch it.

But something in him screamed.

Truth

Was sitting

Inside a locked screen.

They ate in silence.

She scrolled through a new Reel, laughed to herself, and asked him to try a filter on her.

He did.

She looked beautiful.

But the smile he loved was now borrowed — from someone else's attention.

Later, they lay in bed. She lay facing away. He placed a hand on her shoulder, tentative. She didn't react.

He leaned in, softly.

"I love you, Maya," he whispered. She was still. Then she said:

"I know."

No "I love you too." Just... "I know." *That night,*

His heart cracked In a foreign city,

On a borrowed pillow, Next to a woman

Who wasn't really his.

The next morning, she was all cheer again.

"Let's go to Covent Garden. You'll love the performers."

He followed like a shadow.

They clicked photos with flowers and cobbled streets. She posted a carousel — five images.

None had him in it.

That night, he couldn't take it anymore.

After she showered and slipped into bed, he spoke: "Maya… are we okay?"

She turned to him.

"Why do you ask?"

"You feel... far. I came here thinking we'd grow closer. But I feel like you're not really here."

She paused. Looked at him.

Then: "Arjun, I told you I'm not expressive. And London is overwhelming. Stop overanalyzing. Just enjoy what we have."

What we have.

He had love.

She had moments.

She turned away again. He stared at the ceiling. His body was in bed.

His heart was on a plane back to India.

His mind was trapped in the room with her… wondering who she was when she wasn't pretending to love him.

That night, he dreamt of a version of Maya who chose him. Who held his hand. Who kissed him back. Who wasn't texting someone else while lying beside him.

But when he woke up,

She was already packing her bag —

Saying she had a spa appointment alone.

Chapter 11
Two Tickets, One Farewell

"The hardest goodbyes aren't spoken. They happen in silence, while you're still holding their hand."

Day 8 – Cracks in the Cobblestones

Arjun woke up to an empty bed.

Maya was on the armchair, curled like a cat, sipping tea and watching the drizzle outside. Her hair messy, her eyes unreadable.

"You didn't sleep much," he said, his voice still heavy from last night's silence.

"I don't sleep much when I travel," she replied without turning.

"Too many dreams. Too little meaning."

He got up, hoping the morning would reset the mood. "Let's do something today. Walk through Notting Hill. I've heard the Portobello Market is magical."

She nodded. "Sure, if we're not late. I want to check a few stores first. I have to buy something for my brother."

That brother again, Arjun thought.

Shopping Streets and Subtle Betrayals

She led him through boutiques and vintage stores, always seeking something *just right*. A leather wallet. A sleek black watch. A pair of designer shoes.

"He'll love this. He has great taste," she said with a fond smile. Arjun paid.

He didn't mind. Until he saw how softly her fingers caressed the fabric. How she checked the mirror as if visualizing the man who'd wear it — not the one standing beside her, holding the shopping bags.

"Are you sure it's for your brother?" He asked lightly, almost jokingly.

She paused, then laughed.

"Who else, silly? You're getting insecure over a pair of shoes?" Arjun smiled. But something inside twisted.

Afternoon – Love in Public, Loneliness in Private

They clicked pictures at Westminster. A few couple shots she allowed — her hand gently resting on his shoulder. The camera saw two lovers.

But in truth, she flinched at touch. Moved an inch away every time his fingers lingered too long. Her smile was curated. Her eyes wandered to notifications.

At the London Eye, he kissed her on the cheek mid-sunset. She turned toward the glass. "You're so clingy in public."

He didn't reply. He just whispered to himself, *"I thought this was our honeymoon..."*

Night – A Bar Too Loud, A Silence Too Sharp

They visited a rooftop lounge in Soho. Loud music. Expensive cocktails. People dancing too close.

Maya looked stunning — in a black dress that clung to her curves, her lipstick deep red. Men stared. Arjun felt proud. And hollow.

"Want to dance?" He asked.

"I'm tired. You go," she said, sipping her drink.

He stayed beside her. Staring at her face glowing in the club light. She barely noticed.

She was busy texting again.

He asked her about the ring she kept fidgeting with.

She shrugged. "Just a family piece. Heirloom. My mom wants me to pass it to my future husband."

"And who would that be?"

She looked him dead in the eyes.

"Let's not get ahead of ourselves, Arjun."

Return to the Room – A Night that Should Have Meant Something

Back in the hotel, Arjun took her hand gently.

"Maya, I came here because I believed… we were something." She didn't speak.

He kissed her. She kissed back — for a second. Then stopped.

"I can't, Arjun," she whispered. "I'm sorry. I just… I don't feel anything."

"Not even with me?"

"Especially not with you."

Her words sliced through him like ice.

She wrapped herself in the comforter and turned to the wall. "I just want to sleep."

Midnight Thought – Alone Together

Arjun sat at the window, shirtless, staring at the streetlights flickering in the puddles below.

She lay behind him. The same room. The same bed. But miles away.

His journal lay open on the desk. He wrote:

"She wore my hope like a necklace, glittering until it suffocated.

Every gift I gave, she wore for someone else.

Every kiss she took, she saved for memory, but never for love."

Final Blow – The Next Morning

Day 9 began with her packing faster than expected.

"Let's cut the trip short," she said. "My dad's planning my engagement. I need to be back."

"Engagement?" Arjun's voice cracked.

"Oh. I didn't tell you? Sorry. It's just a formality." She avoided eye contact.

"But what about us?" He asked.

"I told you, Arjun. We were just… figuring it out."

"You said this trip was our beginning."

"I never promised anything. You assumed."

He sat frozen.

She walked to the mirror, put on the watch he bought — then took it off.

"No, this one's for him."

Poetic Note: Arjun's Realization

"Theticket said return.

But I left pieces of myself behind.

In store aisles where she smiled for another. In hotel sheets where we didn't become one. In her eyes, that never once looked at me like I mattered."

Chapter 12
Blocked and Broken

"Sometimes the person who broke you is the only one who can explain why. But they never do."

The Return — Only One Came Back

When the plane landed in Mumbai, Arjun felt emptier than when he boarded.

The seat beside him, where Maya once sat, now seemed like the ghost of a dream. She had taken an earlier flight. Alone. No goodbye kiss, no farewell hug. Just a message:

"Don't overthink everything. It was just a trip."

The moment his phone connected to the Indian network, he opened Instagram — hoping to see some sign that she missed him. But instead, he found himself blocked. Everywhere.

WhatsApp. Instagram. Facebook. Even on LinkedIn. She had vanished. As if he never existed.

The Evidence Unfolds

The betrayal wasn't just in what she said — it was in what she wore.

Scrolling through a friend's tagged photos, he saw her. At a dinner party. With a man.

Tall. Smiling. Wearing the same shoes Arjun had paid for in London. The same black watch. The same wallet she insisted was "for her brother."

In the photo, Maya leaned into the man's chest like home. Her caption read: *"Forever begins when lies end."*

The irony burned.

Arjun stared at the screen for hours, unmoving. He zoomed into the watch.

Then the shoes.

Then her smile — the same one he never got to see after the first day of the trip.

The Group Chat Revelation

He messaged a mutual acquaintance a friend from their social circle.

"Is Maya dating that guy?"

The reply came fast.

"Not dating. Engaged. Roka was last week. Didn't she tell you?" Arjun's breath caught in his chest.

Engaged.

While he was still holding her hand in London, she had already pledged herself to someone else.

Nights That Burn

That night, Arjun drank.

Not to forget — but to feel something other than the shame crawling over his skin.

He sat on his terrace with the stars overhead and the journal in his lap.

"I kissed her shadow, loved her ghost, and bought gifts for the man who held her heart."

The pain wasn't just emotional. It was physical.

His chest ached. His lips trembled. He held back tears that no longer needed permission.

She hadn't just used him — she had erased him.

Maya's Messages Resurface (via Archive)

He opened his archived emails.

Among the work updates and casual notes, he found one from her—a month before London:

"Promise me when we go to London, you won't pressure me. I want to feel safe. And slow. This trip means everything."

He had honored that. He had kissed her on the forehead every night and asked for nothing more than truth.

But in return, she gave him silence and a disappearing act.

Voice Notes Never Sent

Arjun recorded ten voice notes to send her.

He deleted every single one. In one of them, he had said:

"You don't owe me love.

But you owed me honesty. You owed me the truth before I booked those tickets. Before I held your hand.

Before I kissed your forehead, thinking you were mine."

The Mirror Scene

He stood before the mirror shirtless, staring at himself. "You fool," he said aloud.

He thought about the day she called him *clingy,* the night she said she felt *nothing,* and the morning she wore that watch — not for him, but for her "brother."

He punched the mirror.

Not to shatter it — but to silence it. Because the reflection mocked him too.

Poetic Note: The Aftermath

"You can't mourn a person who is alive. But you can mourn the version of you that they left behind."

"I was a lover. She was a lesson."

Chapter 13

The Ghosts of Her Goodbye

"She left without a word. But somehow, her silence keeps talking to me."

The Silence That Stayed

Arjun's home never felt emptier.

The curtains, once drawn to filter sunlight, now stayed shut all day. The plants he so lovingly watered withered in a corner, just like his sense of self.

He wasn't crying anymore — not outwardly. He had passed the phase of loud sobs. Now, his grief was a quiet fog. It hovered over him. Everything he touched, remembered her.

The blue coffee mug she once said reminded her of Santorini — unused.

The book she half-read and left on his shelf — still dog-eared at page 41.

Her forgotten bobby pin on the sink edge.

She had left without packing memories, and they haunted him like perfumed phantoms.

The Bed That Never Held Love

He lay in his bed, staring at the ceiling fan.

She had been in this bed. Yet, never in his arms.

He had given her space, respect, patience — the kind of tenderness rarely offered anymore. And yet, she gave him distance. Measured affection. A taste of something always out of reach.

He remembered their nights. The way she'd smooch him gently, like a secret. Then recoil, citing trauma, pain, and ghosts from her past.

"I can't… I'm not like other girls," she'd say.

"I'm asexual," she once whispered, holding his hand like a lifeline. "I was raped by family members. Please understand. It's hard for me to trust."

And Arjun did.

Every. Single. Time.

He held her like a porcelain memory. Never demanding. Never questioning. Only hoping.

Now he wondered — how many others heard those same lines?

His Phone: A Graveyard of Their Story

Every ping on his phone triggered his heart. But it was never her.

So he stopped checking notifications. He buried himself in her archived texts.

"You're the only man I feel safe with."

"Let's grow old together, even if I never marry." "Promise me you'll never stop loving me."

"Don't kiss me now. My mom will suspect something." "I want to do London with you — just us, no lies."

He had bookmarked them like prayers. Now, they read like punchlines in a comedy he never auditioned for.

Her Haunting Presence in Public

One afternoon, he sat at a café near her office.

Every woman with long hair and a handbag twisted his breath.

Every passing giggle — a false alarm.

Then he saw her.

Across the street. In a floral kurti. Smiling into her phone. She looked… happy.

He knew that smile. It wasn't his anymore. Maybe it never was. He wanted to run across and scream, "Why?!"

But he sat frozen. She didn't see him.

Or maybe… she did — and looked away.

Therapy — A Failed Attempt at Unpacking Grief

"Have you tried therapy?" His friend asked.

Arjun booked an appointment.

The therapist asked him, "Do you think she loved you?"

"I think… she loved what I gave her." "And what was that?"

"Sanctuary," he said. "And silence. The kind she could lie into without being questioned."

The Night of the Journal Burn

Weeks passed.

One night, he took out the journal he had written during the London trip — the one filled with poems, promises, and love notes to a woman who never reciprocated.

He set it on fire in a steel bucket on his balcony.

The pages curled. Words turned into ash. But somehow, the pain stayed intact.

Poetic Note – The Haunt

"She didn't break my heart.

She broke my mind's memory of love."

"I don't miss her.

I miss the person I was when I thought she loved me."

An Email Never Sent

He drafted one last email to her:

"Maya,

I loved you with the innocence of someone who believed.

You kissed me like a ghost, but I treated you like a goddess.

I spent my days being enough for someone who never wanted me to be.

You weren't a dream.

You were the lesson I never saw coming."

He stared at the "Send" button. Then deleted the draft.

Some pain doesn't deserve a witness.

A Whisper of Hope

On the 40th day after her vanishing, he met a stranger at a book café.

She wasn't extraordinary. She didn't wear expensive perfume. She didn't quote Rumi or play manipulative games.

But she asked him, "Do you like almond milk in your coffee too?" And for the first time, Arjun smiled.

Not because he loved again. But because he felt alive — even if just for a second.

Chapter 14

The Post-London Life — Learning to Breathe Without Her

"Healing doesn't always look heroic. Sometimes it's just deciding to get out of bed and live again."

Wounds That Didn't Bleed

After the storm of betrayal, Arjun was left standing in the wreckage of what used to be his version of love. The hardest part wasn't that Maya left. It was that she had never truly arrived.

She had always been an illusion — an echo in his arms, a mirage in his mind, a mask in the mirror. And now that illusion had cracked — loudly, violently, and publicly. Yet he still missed her.

Not for who she was — but for who he thought she could be.

Unfollowing Her Memories

Arjun didn’t just unfollow Maya on social media — he unfollowed her from his mind.

He took down the framed photo from his study — the one where she wore a yellow dress and called him “her safe place.”

He donated the scarf she had left behind — the one that once smelled of her shampoo.

He erased the playlist titled “For Us” — and cried when the first few notes of *“All Too Well”* played accidentally in his car.

Healing, he realized, was not a straight road. It was a spiral staircase. Some days he climbed. Other days he circled back to where he started.

Conversations With Himself

He began to write.

Not poetry. Not journals.

Just raw letters to himself.

_“Dear Arjun,

You are not stupid.

You are not naïve.

You just loved louder than most people are used to.”_

_“Dear Arjun,

She didn’t choose you — not because you weren’t worthy, but because you saw her pain, and she saw your patience as weakness.”_

It was cathartic. Slowly, the venom turned to ink. And ink turned into release.

Returning to the Courtroom

His first case after the trip was a property dispute. Nothing romantic about it.

But Arjun wore his black robe with quiet pride.

He stood tall.

He spoke clearly.

He won.

His colleagues cheered. His client thanked him profusely. But even then, he felt hollow — as if the applause was echoing through a tunnel he hadn't left yet.

But he knew one thing: he was still capable. If not of love, then at least of justice.

Maya's Surprise Email

One night, he got an email. Subject line: *"I hope you're well."* From: **Maya**

His hands trembled.

He clicked.

_"I know you must hate me. I don't blame you. I just want to say thank you.

You were kind.

You were safe.

You were everything I needed — and didn't deserve."_

There was no apology.

No explanation.

No remorse.

Just an admission. A breadcrumb. A closure he never asked for but perhaps needed.

He didn't reply.

That was his healing.

The New Woman With Almond Milk

They met again.

The woman from the book café.

Her name was Rhea.

A writer.

Uncomplicated.

Warm eyes.

Soft-spoken.

She didn't rush into conversations. She listened.

She didn't ask him to move on. She just asked if he liked almond milk and wore mismatched socks.

One evening, as they walked near Marine Drive, she said, "You look like someone who lost something valuable."

Arjun nodded. "Yes. But I'm starting to believe I didn't lose it. It was never mine."

She smiled. "That's still grief. But it's honest."

Night of the First Real Laughter

It happened over a silly joke.

Rhea tried imitating a cat meowing at his window. Arjun burst out laughing.

Genuine. Loud. The kind that wrinkles the eyes.

He hadn't laughed like that in months.

And just like that — a crack appeared in the wall around his heart.

Not enough to let someone in, but enough to let light out.

Poetic Note – Recovery Isn't Loud

"Healing isn't a movie montage. It's mornings without her scent. Evenings without her voice.

And nights where you finally fall asleep without checking your phone."

"You don't forget her.

You just stop needing the version of her that never truly existed."

The Final Message to Himself

_"Dear Arjun,

Love broke you.

But you built poetry out of the ashes.

And that is your superpower."_

Chapter 15

Horoscopes Can't Heal What Love Has Left

The first night after returning from London, Arjun couldn't sleep.

The room was dark, but his thoughts blazed like wildfire. Memories of Maya's cold eyes, her complaints, her refusals — and that final moment at Heathrow where she hugged him without warmth, without goodbye — gnawed at his chest like rust on iron.

He scrolled through their old chats, rereading the "I miss you"s she once sent. They felt like borrowed words now. Copied. Rehearsed. Mechanically pasted into a performance that fooled him.

"She loved me once… didn't she?"

That question looped endlessly in his mind, each cycle cutting deeper.

When logic gave him no peace, he turned to what millions do when nothing else works —*faith*.

And so began Arjun's secret pilgrimage — not across continents, but across *beliefs*.

ॐ The Astrologer

It started with a friend's recommendation.

"She's a gifted astrologer. Saved my sister's marriage. You must go," the friend said, handing him a phone number scribbled on a crumpled business card.

The woman sat cross-legged in a sparsely lit room in Dadar, surrounded by celestial charts and sandalwood aroma. Her hair was streaked silver and tied in a loose bun. She didn't smile, just looked at him deeply.

Arjun handed over his birth date and time. And Maya's too. Within minutes, she declared, "You both have strong karmic baggage. Yours is a Moon-Venus clash. Her Rahu is shadowing you."

"What does that mean?" Arjun asked, grasping for something — anything.

"She's your karmic test. You were lovers in a past life. She left you once… she'll leave you again."

Arjun's chest collapsed inward. He didn't want it to be true — but some part of him clung to it.

"If I do remedies, will she love me again?"

"Possibly," she said. "Do a Mangal Shanti and wear an opal on

Friday."

He left with an opal ring, a red thread, and a fragile hope that stars might fix what Maya had broken.

🔮 The Tarot Reader

A week later, he walked into a spiritual center in Bandra.

The reader, a young woman with kohl-lined eyes and a soft voice, shuffled her cards gently.

"Think of your question," she said. Will she ever come back?

He thought it. Loudly. Desperately.

She pulled three cards: *The Moon, The Devil, The Tower.*

Not a word was spoken for a minute.

Then she said, "She's hiding truths. There's manipulation. And you... you're holding on to a ghost."

Arjun flinched.

"But we kissed. We were close. We had something real."

The reader looked at him sadly. "Sometimes illusion tastes real.

That's the danger of Maya — not the woman, but the concept."

His throat tightened. Even the universe was punning his pain.

♂ The Numerologist, The Pundit, and the Godmen

In the days that followed, Arjun met a numerologist in Jaipur who told him to change his spelling on social media.

He met a pundit in Nashik who recommended a *navagraha puja* and made him sit in the sun for three hours chanting mantras.

He tied threads at Siddhivinayak.

He walked barefoot in Shirdi.

He donated to girls' education on a Saturday.

He fasted every Thursday.

He wore a white kurta and slept with rose quartz under his pillow.

And yet… her replies became shorter. Her shopping requests continued.

Her warmth never returned.

The Breaking Point

One evening, he lit a diya and prayed silently.

"God, if she's not meant to stay, at least take this love away from me."

His voice cracked mid-prayer.

His opal ring clinked softly against the floor as he folded his hands tighter.

Tears soaked the corners of his eyes — the kind that come not from pain but exhaustion.

He had done everything.

Astrology. Tarot. Therapy. Energy healing. Self-help books.

Even love letters he never sent.

But Maya's silence was louder than all his efforts combined.

✨ The Realization

He finally understood.

You can chant every mantra.

You can align every planet.

But you can't align someone's heart if it was never meant to beat for you.

Sometimes, God doesn't fix what hurts.

Sometimes, He just shows you it's time to walk away.

💔 Closing Scene

Arjun took off the opal ring that night and placed it in a drawer. He kept the red thread but no longer believed it would save him. He looked at her last message: *"Sorry, I'm too tired to talk. Maybe tomorrow."*

He didn't reply.

He finally slept without praying for her return.

Chapter 16

The Vanishing — Blocked, Broken, Betrayed

It happened on a Monday. The kind of Monday that wears a suit of silence and a tie of confusion.

Arjun had just returned from a court hearing — mentally drained, emotionally numb — when he opened WhatsApp to check if Maya had replied. She hadn't responded to his last three texts. But then again, she rarely did lately.

He tapped her name.

"You can't send messages to this contact."

His throat went dry.

He switched to Instagram.

"User not found."

A chill ran down his spine. He went to Facebook.

She was gone there too.

Just like that, she'd vanished. No fight.

No goodbye.

No explanation.

Only absence.

The Collapse of Illusion

His fingers trembled. He tried calling. The call didn't go through.

He sent a desperate message:

"Maya... are you okay? Did something happen?"

But it didn't deliver.

The woman who once said *"you're the only man I can truly open up to,"* the one who cried about family trauma and sexual assault, the one who had used his chest as a pillow and his money as a wallet... had vanished like a bad actor exiting stage mid-dialogue.

Instagram's Brutal Honesty Three days later, he saw it.

A friend who followed Maya's "brother" sent Arjun a screenshot: Her — smiling in London — arm-in-arm with that man.

He wore the **same shoes** Arjun had paid for.

He had the **same Fossil wallet** Maya had claimed was a Raksha

Bandhan gift.

The **watch** she said was for her "mama" gleamed on his wrist.

The caption?

"New beginnings 💍A"

She was engaged.

And it wasn't to Arjun.

The Body Remembers What the Heart Forgets

The memories rushed in like a flood through a broken dam.

That night in London when she cried in the hotel room saying,

"I don't feel love, Arjun… I'm asexual."

The next day she asked him to carry shopping bags from Harrods. Then giggled for two hours texting her "brother."

He remembered the time he tried to kiss her outside a café.

She'd turned away and whispered, **"Too many people watching. Respect me."**

The same woman now had her tongue out in selfies with her so- called sibling on a boat cruise on the Thames.

Nightmares in Daylight

Arjun cried without noise.

He drank three glasses of wine that night. Not out of habit, but heartbreak.

He stared at his phone screen like it might change reality if he just wished hard enough.

He replayed her voice notes.

"You're my comfort zone."

"I've never met anyone like you."

"If my mom wasn't so strict, I'd live with you."

He began to hate her voice. But he couldn't delete the recordings.

A Letter He Never Sent

Dear Maya,

I bought you perfumes so you'd remember me, you wore them for someone else.

I booked the London trip thinking it would heal us, you used it as your engagement moon.

You called me your soulmate, while texting your lover next to me.

I gave you my trust.

You gave me your shadow.

I'm not angry.

Just… hollow.

Arjun.

The Rage Beneath the Ruins

He started questioning himself. Was he blind?

Was he desperate?

Was love supposed to hurt this much?

He went over every red flag. Every night she cancelled plans. Every lie wrapped in trauma.

Every kiss interrupted by *"I'm not ready yet."*

It wasn't a romance.

It was **fraud** camouflaged as affection.

Poetic Closure

One night, staring at the ceiling, he whispered to himself:

"How do you mourn someone who's still alive?"

Maya wasn't dead.

But the version of her he loved had never existed.

He fell asleep that night with no tears left.

Only silence.

And the faint smell of her perfume still lingering on his bedsheet—a ghostly souvenir of betrayal.

Cliffhanger Ending for Chapter 16

The next morning, Arjun woke up to a private Instagram DM.

From an anonymous account.

Just one message:

"Bro, you're not the first she did this to. You want to talk?"

He stared at the screen.

His healing wasn't beginning.

His unravelling had only just started.

Chapter 17

Maya – The Mirror Without a Reflection

"She wasn't born broken. She was bent quietly, taught to smile through bruises, and later — learned to bend others before they bent her."

Maya Iyer knew how to be loved.

Not in the way fairy tales suggested — not with flowers and honesty and shared laughter over coffee.

She knew how to **pull** love toward her.

She knew how to **ignite desire, earn loyalty, evoke protection**, and most dangerously — how to **never quite give it back.**

And she hadn't always been this way.

She was made.

1. Childhood: Learning Silence

Growing up in a conservative South Indian household, Maya had been the ideal daughter — polite, poised, obedient.

But that wasn't the whole story.

Behind the doors of their neat two-bedroom flat, power was often flexed in whispers. Her mother's control wasn't violent — it was psychological. Disapproval came in silence. Love came in conditions.

The first time Maya cried in front of her mother, she was told: "Wipe your tears. They make you weak. No one respects a crying woman."

The first time she was touched inappropriately — by a visiting uncle during a Diwali celebration — she froze. Not because of the act. But because when she told her mother, the reply was chilling:

"Girls like you need to be careful. Don't tell anyone. You'll ruin our name."

That night, Maya learned something far more terrifying than trauma.

She learned that **truth had no value** unless it was **convenient**.

2. College: Discovering Her Power

By the time Maya was in her early twenties, studying finance and interning with an investment firm, she had developed a subtle shield.

She wore elegance like armor.

She learned to be the girl who shared *"just enough pain"* to make men feel special — like they were the only ones who saw the real her.

There was Vikrant, the CFA tutor who let her skip fees.

Rishabh, the mentor at her internship who "rescued" her from office gossip.

Anirudh, the startup founder from Bangalore who offered her a flexible compliance job so she wouldn't have to travel far from home.

Each of them thought they were helping her heal. They didn't realize they were **fueling her strategy**.

3. Early Career: Crafting the Persona

Maya's first full-time job in banking came with power— and male attention.

She was sharp. No question.

But it wasn't just her knowledge of regulatory frameworks that drew senior VPs toward her.

It was the way she carried tragedy.

"I'm not like others. I don't go to parties. I've seen too much." "Relationships scare me. People use you and leave. I don't believe in casual love."

She wasn't playing the victim.

She was playing the *survivor.*

Men didn't desire her because she was broken. They desired her because they thought they could fix her. Save her. Love her *back to life.*

And she let them try.

Every time.

4. The Pattern Emerges

Her process, by now, was methodical:

1. **Choose a man who craved emotional purpose.** The ones who didn't just want sex or success — but *a story.*

2. **Give him an entry point.** A wound. An emotional whisper. A shared trauma — real or curated.

3. **Keep physical closeness ambiguous.** She would kiss, hold, moan softly, but stop just before intimacy. That delay made her unforgettable. Made men ache.

4. **Maintain scarcity.** Meet occasionally. Cancel often. Reply late. But *never* let him feel ignored.

5. **Receive. Always receive.** Dinners. Rides. Books. Bags. Vacations. Emotional labor. Financial favors. Sympathy. Never ask outright—just sigh the right way. They'd offer.

6. **Disappear without warning.** Block. Move cities. Change jobs. A new profile. A new man. A new beginning.

5. The Upgrade: Vashikarana

It was during a silent retreat near Pune that Maya learned about **vashikarana** — an ancient Indian concept once used in tantric rituals to attract, influence, control.

It wasn't sorcery.

It was science — of attention.

The instructor spoke about:

- Breathing patterns that could anchor desire.
- Eye contact that made people lean in unconsciously.
- The right pauses between words.
- Whispering vulnerability like it was sacred.

Maya didn't become evil that day. She became... *efficient.*

6. Enter Arjun

When Arjun Mehra commented on her LinkedIn post, she almost ignored it.

Another well-dressed senior lawyer in his 40s. Another "intellectual savior" type.

But his response intrigued her.

He wasn't flirtatious. He was precise. Honest. Kind.

She tested the waters.

A few emotional lines. A photo late at night. A whispered voice note about her past. He didn't flirt back. He listened.

And that's when she knew — *he wasn't after her body.*

He was after her broken soul.

The perfect prey.

She didn't expect Arjun to give so much.

She didn't expect him to **book London**, to **decorate a hotel suite**, to **cry silently when she said she couldn't go further.**

He was more than the others. More generous.

More vulnerable.

More… poetic.

And that's what made her fear him.

Because Arjun *might've been the only one* who could've reached her.

So she ran. Blocked him. Rewrote the story.

Engaged another man — one who didn't ask questions. And slept peacefully the next night.

7. The Night No One Saw

But weeks later, lying beside her fiancé in silence… Maya opened a drawer.

Inside was a printed photo. Of her in that hotel bathrobe.

Beside a cake.

With Arjun.

She stared at it.

Not for love.

Not for guilt.

But for the echo of something she had long buried —

The version of herself that almost... stayed.

She closed the drawer. And smiled.

Chapter 18
The Confrontation — Final Words Never Spoken

The message sat there, still unread. Arjun had seen it three times, swiped it away twice, and each time it pulled him back like gravity.

“Bro, you’re not the first she did this to. You want to talk?”

From a profile with no name. Just an image of a cracked mirror as the display picture.

He finally typed:

“Who are you?”

The response came in under ten seconds.

“Someone who got played before you. Maya has a pattern.”

The Stranger's Story

Arjun's heart thudded.

The stranger introduced himself as "R," a senior banker based in Singapore. He had dated Maya two years before Arjun.

Same beginning. Same sweet words. Same trauma stories.

Same promises.

Same sudden withdrawal. Same lies.

"She told me she was asexual too. Said she was 'healing from childhood abuse'.

I paid her rent for 3 months. She said she'd return it when her bonus came.

She disappeared. I saw her at a Dubai wedding with another guy two months later."

"I messaged you because… I saw the London pictures. I know those shoes. I bought her the same ones.

She just changes cities. But the script is the same."

Cracks in the Glass

Arjun felt sick.

Everything made sense now — the rehearsed sob stories, the curated innocence, the emotional push-pull.

She wasn't a broken soul trying to heal.

She was a master puppeteer pulling strings while pretending to be the marionette.

He went back to his saved chats, rereading them not as a lover but as a lawyer — dissecting each line like cross-examination.

She never gave timelines.

She avoided specific questions.

Every answer was slippery — wrapped in emotion, dipped in guilt-tripping.

It wasn't love.

It was performance.

Final Attempt

Still… still…

Something in him wasn't ready to let go without one last try. Call it ego.

Call it love's final gasp.

He emailed her from an old ID:

"Maya, just one meeting. No drama. No blame. Just clarity. I need closure. You owe me that much."

She didn't reply.

But two days later, he received a message on Telegram.

"I think it's better if we both move on. Meeting won't help. I've made peace with things. Hope you can too. All the best always."

That was it.

No apology.

No acknowledgment.

Just detachment, neatly typed.

The Message He Never Sent

He wrote back.

But never hit send.

"You don't get to leave like this.

You don't get to use someone's kindness as currency.

You don't get to rewrite the story as if I was just a page you folded and forgot.

I gave you my love. My time. My truth. You gave me your rehearsals.

But thank you.

Because from you, I learned what love should never feel like."

He saved the draft. Then deleted it.

A New Kind of Silence

The silence this time didn't scream. It didn't ache. It… observed.

He didn't cry.

He didn't text.

He didn't spiral.

Instead, he did something unfamiliar —

He sat with his pain, and let it be.

Rebirth in Fragments

He walked barefoot on the beach that Sunday morning. Waves came and went — uncaring of names, losses, betrayals.

He thought about everything Maya had taken: Money. Trust. Months of sleepless nights.

But she hadn't taken his essence.

She hadn't dimmed his capacity to love — just to expect it blindly. And maybe… that was something.

The Final Dream

That night, he had a dream.

He was back in London, standing on the bridge.

Maya walked toward him — wearing the same white dress from that evening at Covent Garden.

But this time, she was transparent — like mist. She smiled, touched his hand…

And then dissolved into smoke. He didn't chase her.

He just stood still.

Letting go.

Chapter 19
Sweetheart. Scandalous. Scammer.

There are scars people see.

And then there are the ones people live inside.

Arjun had stopped explaining himself to others. Because how could he?

How do you explain a heartbreak that didn't even look like one from the outside?

There was no public breakup.

No photographs to burn.

No relationship status to change.

No closure text that marked a beginning of healing.

It was a relationship that began in whispers… and ended in silence. And yet, it broke him — not once, but a thousand times in the quiet.

Labels That Lie

He once called her "sweetheart." She once called him her "only soul."

But in hindsight, the real title she wore was something else.

"Sweetheart. Scandalous. Scammer."

Not in the sense of a thief of money — but a thief of time, of truth, of tenderness.

A scammer of trust.

A manipulator of emotion.

She sold dreams like discount perfume — intoxicating at first whiff, toxic the moment it settled.

Love, Rewritten

Arjun had loved her honestly.

Every smile she smiled, he believed.

Every trauma she claimed, he wanted to heal.

Every excuse she made, he forgave — because he thought love was endurance.

But now, in the afterglow of the storm, he saw clearly.

Love is not pain endured.

Love is truth embraced.

And what they shared… wasn't love. It was illusion. Dressed as intimacy.

The Arjun Who Remained

He didn't become bitter. He became better.

Not immediately — but through slow, silent rebirth.

There were nights he replayed her laughter like a haunted soundtrack.

Mornings he checked his phone instinctively, only to find the same void.

Afternoons he saw something she had touched — a watch, a book, a cup — and it stung.

But every day, the sting hurt less.

Because the Arjun who remained wasn't the one who begged.

He was the one who rebuilt.

Lessons in Ruins

She taught him how dangerous empathy can be when it's given without boundaries.

She taught him that people can fake trauma as a mask — not to heal, but to hide.

She taught him that not everyone who says "I love you" knows what love even means.

But most of all, she taught him how to walk away —
When his soul was screaming to stay.

To the Ones Like Her

This chapter is not revenge.

It is not wrath.

It is not a courtroom verdict.

It is simply a mirror.

To the ones who play with love like a card game — may you one day meet someone who holds up a mirror instead of a rose.

May you feel what it means to be discarded without warning.

To be seen through, not looked at.

To be loved in a way that forces you to confront yourself.

And To the Ones Like Arjun

To the ones who gave too much — Who believed too blindly —

Who forgave too easily — And still, stood back up:

This chapter is your closure.

You are not foolish. You are not weak. You are not a mistake.

You are a lesson someone else couldn't carry.

You are a heart that still dares to beat with hope.

And someday — not in longing, but in laughter — you'll meet someone who doesn't confuse your gentleness for weakness.

Poetic Closure

She was a storm. He was a shelter. She left wreckage.

He built a lighthouse.

And that is how this story ends. Not with revenge.

Not with regret. But with revelation.

Epilogue
The Man Who Learned to Stay with Himself

Months had passed since London. Arjun no longer scrolled through her photos or replayed her voice notes at night. The silence that once suffocated him now felt like space — space to breathe, to rebuild, to rediscover.

He began journaling again, but not about her. His pages spoke of sunsets, friendships rekindled, victories in court, and the surprising lightness of solitude. Therapy helped him unlearn the belief that being "too good" was a flaw. Meditation reminded him that closure is not given by others — it is built within.

When he walked along Marine Drive now, he didn't carry the weight of betrayal. He carried the quiet pride of someone who had survived it. The scam had taken his trust, but it had also given him wisdom: love is not a transaction, it is a choice — and the first person worthy of that choice is yourself.

He no longer waited for Maya's ghost to leave his mind. He simply outgrew her.

Acknowledgements

I owe this book to every soul who has loved with reckless faith and walked away carrying invisible scars.

To my family and friends, who believed in my voice even when my pages were blank — thank you for your patience, encouragement, and quiet strength.

To my mentors, readers, and critics who shaped my words with their honesty — your feedback was my compass.

And finally, to every reader holding this book — you are not alone in your heartbreak, and you are stronger than the storms you have survived.

Reader's Reflection Page

Dear Reader,

This story is not mine. It is a tapestry woven from the stories of different characters and experiences I have witnessed through my journey as a professional, a tarot reader, and a psychic. Their echoes, patterns, and lessons inspired me to bring this narrative alive. My time with Toastmasters helped me shape these fragments into a voice that could reach you with clarity, empathy, and impact.

Take a moment to reflect:

Have you ever ignored red flags because hope felt easier?

Have you mistaken manipulation for love?

What does healing look like for you?